When a Zeeder Met a Xyder

Malachy Doyle

Illustrated by Joel Stewart

DOUBLEDAY

Once upon a mountain
Stood a Xyderzee,
And he said to a goat,

"Oh, woe is me,
I'm a lonely Xyderzee.
Am I the only Xyderzee
In all the world?"

When a
Zeeder
Met a
Xyder

for Liz, with a twinkle
M.D.

For E.P.
& the one in the hat
J.S.

Once, by the sea,
Was a Zeederzoo,
And she asked a slippy trout,

*"What can I do?
I'm a lonely Zeederzoo.
Am I the only Zeederzoo
There is?"*

So the Xyder waved goodbye
To the goat so high,
And he scampered down the hill
Towards the sea.

And the Zeeder packed her bag
And she climbed, zigzag,
Up the path
Towards the Xyderzee.

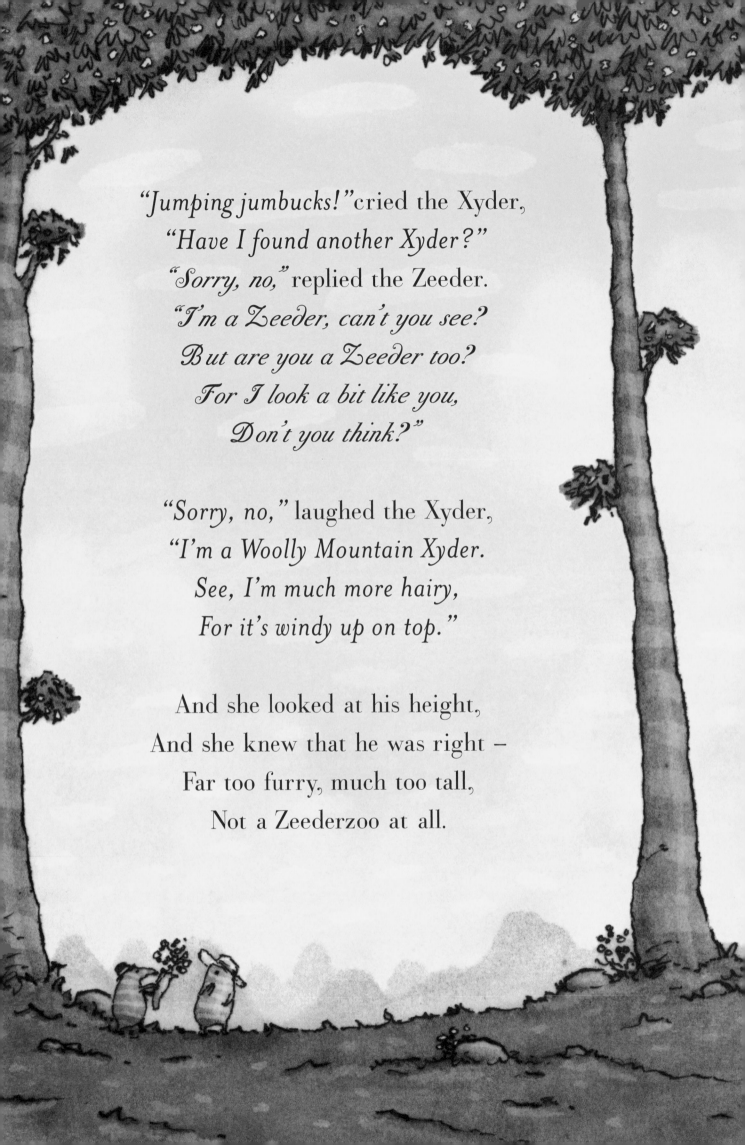

"Jumping jumbucks!" cried the Xyder,
"Have I found another Xyder?"
"Sorry, no," replied the Zeeder.
"I'm a Zeeder, can't you see?
But are you a Zeeder too?
For I look a bit like you,
Don't you think?"

"Sorry, no," laughed the Xyder,
"I'm a Woolly Mountain Xyder.
See, I'm much more hairy,
For it's windy up on top."

And she looked at his height,
And she knew that he was right –
Far too furry, much too tall,
Not a Zeederzoo at all.

So the Xyder bounced along,
Till he reached the salty sea.
And he asked the slippy trout,
"Have you seen a friend for me?"
"Yes, I think so," said the fish.
"She's just gone walking, up the hill."

And the Zeeder climbed and clambered
Till she reached the mountain top,
Where she asked the billy goat,
"Seen anyone like me?"

And the goat said,
"Yes, he's off to find
You by the sea."

"*A friend for ME!*" cried the Xyder,
"*Whoopy-dee!*"

"*One for me!*" sighed the Zeeder.
"*Zippy-zee!*"

And they thought how good it could be,
Dreamed all night how good it would be,
With a Zeeder for a Zeeder
And a Xyder for a Zee.

They jumped up next morning
And ran off to search again.
One hurried up the hill,
The other toddled down the lane . . .
Until they met.

"Jumping jerkins!" cried the Xyder
To the Zeederzoo, "It's you!
I'm still looking for my friend."
"Me too,
And I'm told he's
On the mountain,"
Said the Zeeder to the Xyder.
"That's odd," replied the Xyder.
"For my one's by the sea."

"What's she like?"
Asked the Zeeder.
"I suppose . . ."
Replied the Xyder,
"She'll be tall
And green and hairy,
Just like me."

"Not like me, then?"
Asked the Zeeder.
"Small and bald
And rather blue?"
"No, I'm sorry,"
Said the Xyder,
"Not like you."

"*How about we look together?*"
Said the Zeeder to the Xyder.
"*Good idea,*" replied the Xyder,
And he took her by the hand.

They skipped down to the sea.
The tide was out.
"*Seen my friend?*" asked the Zeeder.
"Round about," winked the trout.

So they ran, clip-clop,
Up to the mountain top.
"Is she here?" gasped the Xyder.
"Very near," said Mister Goat.
"Oh, I'm never going to find her!"
Cried the Xyder. *"What a pain!"*
"How annoying," sighed the Zeeder,
"Missed again!"

But then she looked him in the eye
And saw a twinkle.
And he looked her in the eye
And saw a twinkle twinkling back.
Suddenly they didn't care
If one had longer hair, was taller,
One had shorter hair, was smaller,
One was Zeeder, one was Xyder;
No, what mattered was inside her,
Inside him, and that was something
New and special, something rare.

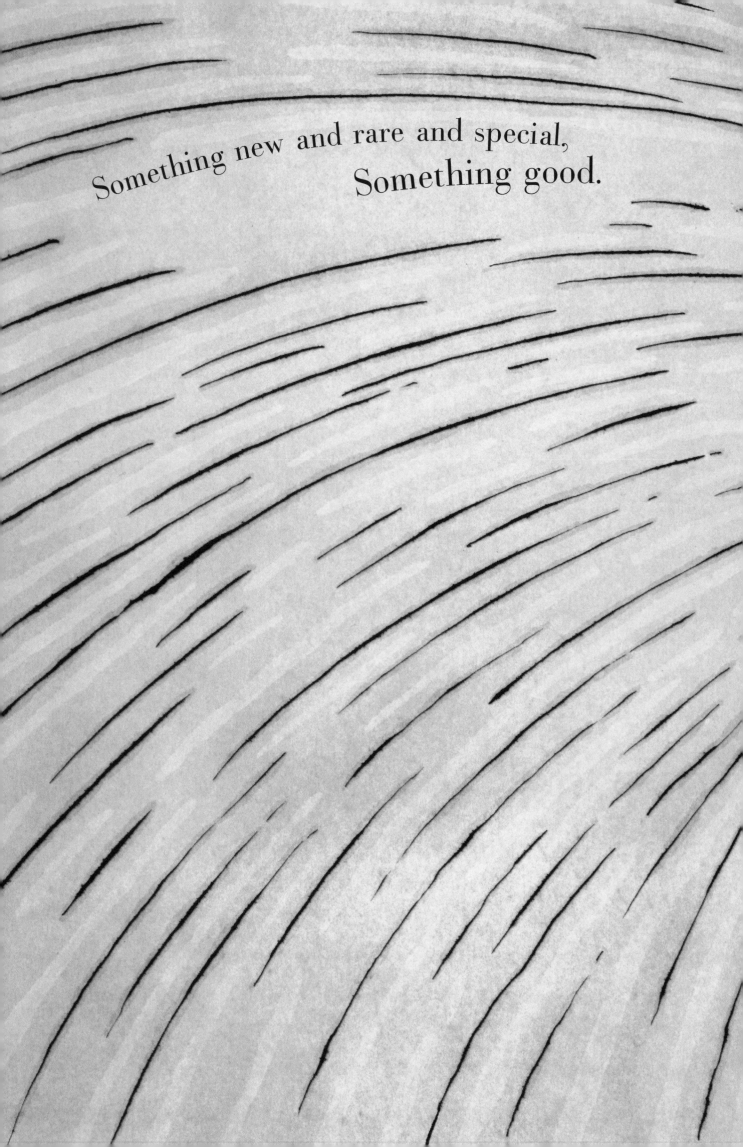

Something new and rare and special,
Something good.

And now the Xyderzee and Zeeder
Live together by the lake.
Never lonely, as they've only
Thirty-seven little Xyderzeeders.
Baldy ones, hairy ones,
Noisy ones and scary ones,
Blue ones, green ones,
Dirty ones and clean ones,
Bouncy ones, sleepy ones,
Growly ones and peepy ones.
Thirty-seven happy little
Xyderzeeder tots.

They didn't
Find a friend . . .

They found

LOTS!

WHEN A ZEEDER MET A XYDER
A DOUBLEDAY BOOK 0 385 60793 8

Published in Great Britain by Doubleday,
an imprint of Random House Children's Books

This edition published 2006

1 3 5 7 9 10 8 6 4 2

Text copyright © Malachy Doyle, 2006
Illustrations copyright © Joel Stewart, 2006

The right of Malachy Doyle and Joel Stewart to be identified as the author and illustrator
of this work has been asserted in accordance with the Copyright, Designs and Patents Act 1988.

RANDOM HOUSE CHILDREN'S BOOKS
61–63 Uxbridge Road, London W5 5SA
A division of The Random House Group Ltd

RANDOM HOUSE AUSTRALIA (PTY) LTD
20 Alfred Street, Milsons Point, Sydney,
New South Wales 2061, Australia

RANDOM HOUSE NEW ZEALAND LTD
18 Poland Road, Glenfield, Auckland 10, New Zealand

RANDOM HOUSE (PTY) LTD
Endulini, 5A Jubilee Road, Parktown 2193, South Africa

THE RANDOM HOUSE GROUP Limited Reg. No. 954009
www.kidsatrandomhouse.co.uk

A CIP catalogue record for this book is available from the British Library.

Printed and bound in Singapore